Another Kind Of Hunger

AMY LAURENS

OTHER WORKS

Find other works by the author at
www.amylaurens.com

Another Kind of Hunger

INKLET #1

AMY LAURENS

Inkprint PRESS

www.inkprintpress.com

Print ISBN: 978-1-925825-01-5
eBook ISBN: 9781386389415

www.inkprintpress.com

*National Library of Australia Cataloguing-in-Publication
Data*
Laurens, Amy 1985 –
Another Kind Of Hunger
52 p.
ISBN: 978-1-925825-01-5
Inkprint Press, Canberra, Australia
1. Young Adult Fiction—Fantasy 2. Young Adult
Fiction—Short Stories 3. Young Adult Fiction—
Family 4. Young Adult Fiction—Boys & Men

First Print Edition: January 2019
Cover design © Inkprint Press
Interior art © Amy Laurens

****WARNING****
Contains mild plot spoilers for
Through Roads Between, Sanctuary #2.

ANOTHER KIND OF HUNGER

Scott waited for the usual shouts of irritation to greet him as he slammed the front door of his home and kicked his black school shoes off. Instead, silence hovered over the house, heavy and cloying. Silence, that was, except for his rumbling stomach. He sighed and schlepped down to his room, dodging the stacks of miscellaneous paperwork and clothing in various states of cleanliness that lined the hallway. Looked like dinner would be beans on toast again.

Scott kicked open the door to his room and crossed the threshold into sanity. The rest of the house was his mother's domain, carpets crusted with dirt and crumbs and ineffectual insect spray, mould growing in the corners where damp had invaded the house, drains stinking like a public toilet block.

In his room, the carpet was, if not clean, at least vacuumed. The array of stains were at least assured to stay where they were, and the walls had been scrubbed down so regularly they were starting to look worn. He closed the door with a heavy sigh and dumped his school bag in the bottom of the wardrobe.

Undressing was an exercise in precision: trousers washed only two days ago meticulously folded for reuse tomorrow, sweat-infused shirt in the hamper, tie over the hanger in the wardrobe. He pulled on trackies that would have crushed his carefully cultivated reputation in one fell swoop if anyone from school ever saw them, and a t-shirt that had sprouted at least two new holes since he'd worn it last time. There was a uniform free day coming up next week; he'd have to raid Mum's wallet again.

Out in the kitchen, three envelopes skulked on the bench, all addressed to his mother, all unopened. Scott glanced at them. Phone bill, electricity and water. He rubbed a hand up his face, under his glasses and over his eyes. Dammit. The welfare payment wouldn't be banked for another ten days. He'd have to call Aunt Sally again.

Whatever. Problem for later. Right now, the most pressing problem was his gurgling stomach. Lunch had been good old air yet again—easy to hide with enough arrogance and a few simpering girls to hold people's attention—and it was nearly half past five.

He opened the pantry door and was halfway through reaching for a can of baked beans before his brain registered the shadows. *What the hell?* He clenched his jaw, hands fisted. This was just too far.

Heat settled in Scott's stomach as he stalked into the laundry. The rancid air made his eyes tear, but that was just another fact of life. He scooped a mouse out of the writhing tank in the corner—he'd long since gotten used to the feel of ten mice trying to cling tooth and claw to his arm at once—and shoved the wretched thing in his pocket. It squeaked in anguish as something broke—but he'd long stopped caring about that, too. He had the best role model in the world for not caring, after all.

But shadows, right there in the kitchen? Right where his mediocre dinner was supposed to be? Okay, so the house had more in common with a trash heap than a home. Okay, so she was often caught up in her mindless little schemes and forgot to make food. But *shadows*? In the *kitchen*? His cheek began a little twitching routine as he flung the pantry doors open again and surveyed the damage. Damn it all, he was hungry.

Scott fought down the disgust building in his chest. He should wait, be cautious and sensible, go down to the stream and cross over properly.

His stomach rumbled. Screw sensible.

He grabbed at the mouse, hardened against its pain by years of practice, and set it under his hand on the shelf, right near the edge of the shadows. Did he dare?

His stomach rumbled again, not so much a gurgle of hunger as a tight knot of emptiness. Gritting his teeth, Scott shoved the mouse towards the shadows with both hands. He closed his eyes and at the last instant, just as he felt the first brush of darkness, he snapped the mouse's neck.

It wasn't a terribly difficult thing to do; just about as difficult as breaking a paddle pop stick.

And imagining it was just a stick helped with the guilt later. Just a little guilt—four hundred and sixty-three mice previously were enough to dull the edges of it—but he added another one to the tally even as he imagined the Valley in crisp detail, eucalypts with their flashing leaves dancing in the wind, the smell of dirt and hard rock, the sharp-edged tussock grass, the heavy, cloying heat.

His body twisted towards the place, and he flung out a hand, catching at the darkness he sensed behind him— and Scott popped into the Valley, dragging a fistful of shadows. He flung them away and wiped his hand on his shirt.

In only took a minute to dig a grave deep enough for the mouse, and then he was off.

He knew where she'd be; she never went far and, coming around the corner of a hill, Scott saw the billowing pillar of darkness his mother called home.

It still made his neck itch.

Muttering idle threats to himself, he marched towards it, hardly even hesitating as he plunged from broad, sunless daylight into all-consuming black.

"Mum? Are you in here?"

A laugh that was only half delighted rang out. "Scott, darling? What a lovely surprise."

Hands fisting at his sides, Scott marched closer. The pillar, only a couple of paces across from outside, had been steadily growing in breadth inside every time he'd entered it; now it took him no less than thirty long strides to reach the centre of the darkness, where his mother luxuriated beneath a twisting, spiralling column of light.

"Seriously?" he muttered, glancing up at it.

"Isn't it lovely, dear?"

The look on his mother's face bordered on rapturous, and Scott sighed. "Yeah. Sure, Mum. It's lovely. But—"

Scott Harden? a voice boomed in his head. *Do you also come to me?*

Scott blinked. "Uh, Mum?"

She tittered. "Isn't it simply marvellous?"

He eyed the pillar with suspicion, hunger momentarily forgotten. "What *is* it?"

His mother turned to face him for the first time, eyes alight. "This is the Valley, Scott," she said, voice sharper and more lucid than he'd heard it in weeks.

"I know we're in the Valley, but—"

"No! This *is* the Valley." She turned back to the twisting pillar of light.

"This is the heart of its power, made sentient, given life."

Scott eased himself a little further away. *Crazy lady at two o'clock. Okay then.* "That's… That's great, Mum. You did this?"

She beamed, even as the voice lashed out at his thoughts. *No,* it said. *I have done this thing. I am will, I am power; she is merely the life force I required.*

Scott frowned. Life force? That sounded… permanent. "Uh, Mum? You sure this is a good idea?"

It wasn't, obviously; her ideas rarely were. But this seemed stupid on a more spectacular level than usual.

"Now, Scott," she chided, taking his hand and tucking it into the crook of her arm. "Don't you want something nice to eat?"

He snatched his hand back. "Funny you should say that, considering all the *shadows* where the *food* should be in our pantry."

While he'd spoken, his mother had positioned herself behind him, and now she took him by the shoulders and forced him forward, towards the pillar of light.

"Mum, I'm serious! You can't keep messing around with these things. We can barely afford to eat as it is, and if you d—" The word died in his throat and he swallowed down the sudden burn of grief.

He shook his head.

His mother squeezed his shoulders and pulled him close against her chest. "Hush, now dear. Don't you think I know that? Why else do you think I did this? Can't you imagine what this much power can offer us?"

He tried to face her, but her iron grip held him fast. "Mum, I—"

"Go, son. Make your peace with the darkness, and you will rule it all."

She shoved him forward and he stumbled, trying desperately to fling himself aside. Instead, he tumbled headfirst into the pillar of light.

He screamed as it swallowed him, light burning through every pore.

So, you come at last, the voice he'd heard before said with satisfaction, louder this time.

Scott spat blood from his mouth, wiped his lips on the back of his hand, and dragged himself to his feet. "No."

No? The light flared around him. *But Scott*—shivers slid over him at the sound of his name, eerily familiar on the light's metaphorical tongue—*you could have so much.*

Images flashed fleetingly through his head: control, order, neatness, everything clean and tidy and organised.

Longing rolled through his body.

He shoved it aside and forced himself to sound nonchalant. "Heh. Not unless you've got dinner in there for me."

He reeled as images of food assaulted his senses: the smell of roasting chicken; potatoes crackling in a buttery pan; bowls dripping with jewel-coloured fruits, sweet and lush; cheeses stacked higher than his hips, creamy-coloured and butter-yellow, veined and holed; the smell of rosemary, savoury and fresh; mint, sharp and sweet; cakes laden with icing and cream, swirled through with jam and curd and chocolate.

"Stop!" he cried, cowering with his hands over his head. His gut wrenched. "Please, just stop!"

All of it, the light crooned. *You could have it all.*

The sensations intensified, his stomach cramping.

"No," Scott whispered, curling tight into a quivering ball. "I am not my mother."

No? the light whispered back. *Are you sure?*

"I'm sure." The words were barely audible, but given he could hear the light in his head, it probably didn't matter.

You refuse? The light's voice roared like lightning. *You refuse* me?

Scott only had time to tense before the burning began again. Knives of pain shot from every inch of his skin, sharp and hot. "Stop!" he screamed—only he couldn't scream, couldn't breathe. Pain poured down his throat, a liquid fire that set his body ablaze. In his head, he screamed, and screamed, and screamed.

Between breaths, he realised that the shouting wasn't all in his head, wasn't all his. "Mum?" he sobbed. "Mum! Help!"

The high-pitched whine of an insect filled his right ear over the roar of the light. It took a decade of effort to raise his arm, cup his hand, terrified the mosquito would fly away. But he must have moved faster than it felt, because he slapped his own temple, capturing the creature, and in the instant its life force drained away, he imagined his mother's den in perfect clarity, and twisted away.

He lay on thin, dusty carpet, wheezing and clutching at his ribs as the fire died away. He couldn't tell if the sounds he was making were sobs or groans or maybe even laughter, because the whole thing was insanity; his mother had cracked, finally, gone mad and nearly dragged him under as well.

He was going to die, cold and hungry and alone.

Sobs. Definitely sobs.

The doorbell rang.

He staggered upright with a monumental effort of will.

His muscles ached and his skin felt raw, but he straightened, exhaled, and cleared the pain from his face. Heaven knew he had enough experience doing that, as well.

A vaguely familiar smell greeted him right before he opened the door, and then he did, and he had to lean against the doorframe to stop himself was falling.

"There's a letter with the delivery," the pizza guy said, holding out one of the cobweb-edged envelopes his mother got specially made.

Pizza. Mum had ordered pizza.

Hand barely shaking at all, he took the envelope. With a crisp, crackling tear, he opened it and withdrew the letter.

"I'm sorry, Scott. It will all be better soon. I promise. I went back a little to get you the pizza—I'm sorry about the pantry—and I'll be home in time for bed. Save me a slice. I love you." The bottom was signed with her initials, and next to it... He let out an explosive exhale that almost sounded like a laugh. She'd sketched a mosquito. It had been her he'd heard after all—she'd sent the mozzie to save him.

Scott closed his eyes and pressed the note against his chest, not even caring that the pizza guy might see the wetness leaking around the corners of his eyes. He appreciated the pizza more than words could say, and she'd saved him from the light, that was true.

But where the shadows had come once, he knew they'd come again, and one day he wouldn't be strong enough to drag them all away. "Dammit, Mum," he told the letter. "It'll never be over. Not ever."

But for now, at least, there was pizza to eat.

THE MAKING OF
ANOTHER KIND OF HUNGER

Some stories are written because they arrive in your head, demanding to be written; some are written with more deliberation as you try to tease out the details of a character or a world.

This story was one of the latter. I wrote it between writing *Sanctuary* books one and two (*Where Shadows Rise* and *Through Roads Between*) because all of a sudden, I needed to get into the head of the boy who'd been my villain, and figure out what was going on there. And believe it or not, this did actually help: just the act of writing from his perspective allowed me to get a better handle on his personality, on the way he worked to hide his private life from everyone else around, and on the complicated relationship he had with his mother.

If you want to see more of Scott, you're in luck! Pick up my *Sanctuary* series to read all about him from a classmate's point of view.

In fact, you can read the first chapter of book one right now, just over the page ☺

DOWNLOAD YOUR FREE EBOOK

When you buy a print book from Inkprint Press, we like to say THANK YOU by offering you the ebook for free!

Please head to www.inkprintpress.com/inklets/1/ and the use the coupon INKLET1 to get your copy of this Inklet in epub AND mobi today!
(Coupon will only work once.)

Read more in this world!

WHERE SHADOWS RISE

CHAPTER ONE

THE DOORBELL RANG. That doesn't sound exciting in and of itself, but let me assure you: it was the most heart-pounding thing to happen all week. It was my birthday, I was home alone, and because of the stupid witness protection business, I'd been stuck in the house all summer. I hadn't even been allowed out to see friends, because we'd arrived in town at the end of last year with only three school weeks to go—so I didn't have any friends.

Well. I had friends, but they were back in Melbourne, and I wasn't allowed to contact them for fear someone would track down our new location. Lucky me.

Anyway, it was my birthday, I was alone because Mum and Dad had gone to do something regarding birthday surprises and Anna had inexplicably chosen to go with them, and the doorbell had just rung. I stared at the closed door, heart pounding, while our chocolate Labrador, Veve, tried to chew it down. Was I going to open it?

Of course I was going to open it. The chances of it being a mobster were slim to none; for starters, a mobster wouldn't have rung the bell.

I opened it.

"Miss Tanning?" The deliveryman raised a questioning eyebrow and cocked a digital pen at me.

I nodded, heart flip-flopping, and scrawled a fair impersonation of my signature on the digital pad.

He handed over a small, brown-paper parcel with a handwritten address, and departed.

I closed the door behind him, throat dry, and stared down at Veve. On the one hand, yay birthday present. On the other, holy crap, someone had our address. That was *not* a good thing.

It became even less of a good thing when I noticed that the parcel was indeed addressed to a Miss Tanning: a Miss *Anna* Tanning, as in my sister, not me, Emma Tanning.

Anger bubbled up in my chest, hot and tight, and the parcel protested in my grip.

Veve whined softly.

"How could she *do* this?" I whispered to Veve.

I turned the parcel over. It was from Kade, Anna's frogging ex-boyfriend. Who apparently wasn't an 'ex' after all.

Urgh. I ground my teeth. "You know what?" I asked Veve.

She looked up at me with her liquid brown eyes, tongue lolling as she smiled.

"Screw it. If Anna can get interstate mail from people who aren't even supposed to know we exist anymore, you and I can go for a walk on my birthday. What do you think?"

They say dogs don't speak English, but Veve sure as heck knew the word 'walk'—though I think in her vocabulary it was something closer to 'Magical Trip To Disneyland' and less like 'Comparatively Bland Meander Through Trees'.

She tucked her tail right under her butt and shot down the hall, whirling in frantic circles a few times at the end before pelting back as I retrieved her lead from the drawer in the front cabinet.

I rolled my eyes as I clipped her lead onto her collar. For my troubles, I got slimed right up the nostrils. "You're disgusting, you know that?" I wiped off the worst of the dog slobber on the shoulder of my shirt. She just grinned.

Out on the street, she leapt and twisted madly. "Hair-brain," I told her, snapping the lead to get her attention. "It's just a walk."

She just snorted—and stiffened. I followed her gaze to where a flock of corellas pecked their way through the dry grass at the end of the street.

"Veve!"

My shout was in vain: the lead burned through my fingers and Veve shot down the road, a chocolate bullet howling death and destruction for all things feathered.

I cursed her to the lower circles of doggie hell. Which probably involved, I don't know, a world devoid of birds, cats, people, sunshine, and walks, if Veve was anything to go by.

"Veve!" If the sight of the mad Lab-rat barrelling toward them hadn't scared the birds off, my shouts would have. "Come back here *now!*"

Predictably, she ignored me, pounding down the slope, through the fringe of gum trees, and down the narrow stairs between giant granite boulders that led to the river.

"Stupid frogging brainless beast of a stupid frogging dog," I muttered as I followed. "If Mum gets home before we do and freaks out, I swear, I'll pluck your tail hairs out."

Empty threats, obviously, but Mum's freak-out wouldn't be. Her thoughts would go straight to the day Anna nearly died—and I wouldn't blame her.

I should have left a note. Urgh.

The stairs ended and I found myself on a track broad enough for two twisting along a creek the colour of bitter tea. Tussock grass clustered in spikes—where the eucalypts would let it—and hot summer sunlight glinted from the leaves. Somewhere to my right, downstream and in the opposite direction to the house, Veve barked. I exhaled like a whale coming up for air and set out after her.

Veve bounded out from the under-growth in front of me, a dolphin leaping through water, tongue flapping with every bound. "Stupid mutt," I told her under my breath.

She didn't care what I thought (of course), and saved a leap for the last minute so she could plant muddy feet on my hips as I tried to catch her collar.

I straightened, about to insult her some more, and realised that she'd gone stiff again, ears pricked and mouth tight, listening down the path.

My neck prickled. Someone was coming. A second later, I heard footsteps in the gravel, and a low, male voice, humming, or maybe singing softly.

My chest constricted, and just as suddenly my hands were slick. Chances were it was just a stranger out for a midday stroll, but my stomach wound knots about my memories and

I smelled the hot concrete and melting asphalt, old oil and stale urine of the Lilydale train station where the body had been hidden in a toilet stall, the body of the girl who'd looked like Anna.

I had to get off the path.

"Come on, Veve," I said, pulling her close, white-knuckled as I stepped into the undergrowth. The tea tree scrub protested, but I shoved my way through anyway, glancing over my shoulder as the humming grew louder.

I kept going until I couldn't hear footsteps any more, until the wind swallowed the hum that sounded too like the warning cry of a hive—danger, we're working here, come close and get stung. I didn't want to get stung; visions of a blood-streaked face refused to be blinked away.

Only Veve tugging brought me back to myself, and I realised firstly that I was holding the lead way too tight, cutting off Veve's air supply, secondly that the reason my cheeks were suddenly cold was because I'd been crying, and thirdly that I'd found the creek again, looping back parallel maybe fifty meters or so from the path.

Abruptly, I dropped Veve's lead and strode forward to kneel by the water. I dipped my hands in. A shiver slid through me at its chill, and I scooped it up to wash my face.

Flinging the excess water away, I gulped at the air, deep, calming breaths all the way down into my belly, and visualised a river washing away the blood from my thoughts, just like the police psych had taught me.

Once the space behind my eyes was calm and black, I drew in one last forceful breath, and opened my eyes. Perched on a rock by the creek, I hugged my knees to my chest as cool water lapped at my toes. Veve was a little upstream, just before the creek bent back toward the path, doggy paddling in circles in a deep spot where the water broadened to maybe ten meters across. In front of me it was broad but shallow, only ankle deep, its path torn to white foam by the rocks.

And—I gasped. In the middle of the stream, glittering in the sun like a piece of fallen sky, was the hugest butterfly I'd ever seen.

Which was pretty huge; besides the fact that I grew up visiting the Melbourne Zoo with its impressive butterfly house every Christmas since I could remember, Mum and Dad had taken us up to Brisbane for a family holiday two years ago, and we'd seen giant tropical butterflies bigger than my hand.

This one, bright blue with black edging like a Ulysses, was bigger than both my hands put together.

And then it turned around.

Okay. I'd grown up reading fairy tales as much as the next person, and although I'd had a horse-crazy stage instead of a fairy-crazy stage like Anna had, I'd seen all her paraphernalia.

Still, none of it prepared me for finding something that looked exactly like a fairy, standing smack in the middle of a creek in boring, back-water Nowra.

I'm pretty sure my eyes were only hanging in their sockets by a thread.

And then it talked.

Her face lit up like a cloud had just uncovered the sun as she spotted me. "Hi there!" she said, fluttering over.

I just stared, heart pounding against my ribcage as though it wanted to run away from the absurdity of it all. "No," I said. "I'm hallucinating."

The fairy frowned. "I don't think so."

I shook my head. "No. No, things like this do not happen. Things like this aren't *real*." I stood, backing up a step.

The fairy sighed. "I promise. I'm quite real."

"You would say that, wouldn't you," I said, eyeing her. "Veve!" I waved at the dog and hopped from one foot to the other, trying to lure her in with the promise of play. "We're going now!"

Veve, adorable beast that she was, landed a little upstream and shook vigorously before trotting toward me. I backed hurriedly away from the bank, dancing to keep Veve's attention.

"Wait!" the fairy cried, wings snapping out and propelling her a couple of feet into the air. "You're a Traveller! I need to talk to you!"

"Uh huh, sure," I said as I wound the lead around my hand and set off back into the bushes. This was punishment for leaving the house, obviously. The universe was out to get me, reminding me forcefully that once you started disregarding some rules, who knew what other rules you'd end up flouting.

The rules of physics, for example.

I glanced back once, right before the bushes hid the stream altogether. Blue flashed, high up, but I ducked to get a better view and it was only the sky. I scowled. Stupid fairy. Stupid universe. Served me right for leaving the house in the first place. Urgh. "Come on, Veve," I said, snapping the lead. "Even if the house is prison, at least it's *sane*."

I was stomping so furiously as I burst out onto the path that when a figure rose from a stoop only a couple of steps away, I squeaked in surprise.

I scowled. People rarely surprised me; usually I could tell without trying that someone was near. I really must have been off in my own little world.

I glowered at the boy who lived to make my school life a misery. "What are you doing here?" I snapped. "Isn't it bad enough that I have to deal with you on school days? Which, by the way, don't start until tomorrow. You're ruining my holidays."

Okay, so maybe that was a little harsh, but come on. It was *Scott*. I'd arrived in town with three weeks left in the school year, and he'd spent every day of them humiliating me in front of his mates, and I didn't care for a repeat this year.

Scott eyed me warily, which was a strange expression on him.

Usually he strode around like he knew without a doubt that he was too good for the world, and also—somewhere deeper, somewhere I'd only caught a glimpse of once or twice—that it had nothing left to throw at him that could hurt.

Occasionally, in my more generous moments, I wondered what had happened to make him look that way.

Mostly, however, I just wondered why he was such a moron.

"What are you doing here?" he asked, voice dripping with accusation and suspicion.

My hands fisted of their own accord, and beside me Veve's hackles rose as she chimed in with a low-pitched, rumbling growl. I flicked the free end of the lead at her nose. "Nothing," I said, in a rousing blaze of wit. "What are you doing?"

He scowled. "You shouldn't be here."

For one heart-stopping instant I thought he meant out here generally, walking around, as if he knew what had happened and why I'd hidden away all summer. Then I realised he was nodding into the undergrowth. I rolled my eyes. "I might be a city slicker," I bit off, "but I'm not stupid. I made enough noise to scare off a herd of elephants, let alone any snakes that might have been lying around." The thought chilled me, though; I *hadn't* been thinking about snakes when I'd hurried off the path. One badly-timed footstep and a brown snake bite later, and I could be a dead body too.

But Scott had moved on, stalking off down the path. He had nice shoulders, I'd give him that much. Pity he couldn't derive his personality from them, instead of whatever dead weight it was he kept inside his head for brains.

Beside me, Veve growled again, louder this time, more urgent. I snapped the lead at her and stared after Scott's retreating form, trying to think of something cutting.

It was only when Veve growled for the third time that I realised she wasn't even facing Scott. Instead, she was looking back into the bushes—and something dark was flickering in there, deep in the shadows of the trees.

My chest squeezed in on itself and adrenalin shot through my body. Veve's growling grew louder until it broke in a bark, something midway between slavering and terrified, and I realised my tongue was stuck to the roof of my mouth. Carefully I peeled it away, unable to tear my eyes from the shifting darkness in the bushes. There was no discernible form, just shadow, darker than it should have been this soon after midday, and a pervasive sense of dread clamping down on me like an on-coming storm.

Veve began backing away, hackles prickling, growl rising and falling like thunder. I glanced down at her, back to the shadows—and they were closer, much closer than they had been.

I turned and bolted.

Keep reading! Head to
[http://www.amylaurens.com/book s/sanctuary/where-shadows-rise/](http://www.amylaurens.com/books/sanctuary/where-shadows-rise/)
to buy your copy now!

ABOUT THE AUTHOR

AMY LAURENS is an Australian author of fantasy fiction for all ages. She has never seen a fairy or travelled to Sanctuary (sadly), but she has definitely owned a Labrador almost exactly like Veve (though Amy's Labrador was yellow, not brown).

In addition to the *Sanctuary* series of portal fantasy stories set in Nowra, Australia, Amy has written the humorous fantasy series *Kaditeos: Mercury,* beginning with *How Not To Acquire A Castle,* as well as a whole bunch of non-fiction for writers and non-writers alike.

You can find out more about Amy at her website, www.amylaurens.com.

INKLET #007
SEVENTY
LIANA BROOKS

INKLET #008
A Final Request
for Mercy
AMY LAURENS

INKLET #009
the kitten psychologist
vs.
the kitten's owners
THEA VAN DIEPEN

INKLET #010
Answer the
Question
AMY LAURENS

INKLET #011
Happily,
Red
AMY LAURENS

INKLET #012
the kitten psychologist
tries to be patient
through email
THEA VAN DIEPEN

INKLET #013
DRAGON
Tuesday
AMY LAURENS

INKLET #014
RED PLANET
REFUGEES
LIANA BROOKS

INKLET #015
the kitten psychologist &
What The Kitten Did
THEA VAN DIEPEN

Cherry Blossom
AMY LAURENS

Alone
AMY LAURENS

the kitten psychologist
& The Kitten
Come To A Conclusion
THEA VAN DIEPEN

LEVEL NINE
LIANA BROOKS

To Dust
AMY LAURENS

Interchange
AMY LAURENS

Emalia's Lanterns
LIANA BROOKS

Dear Santa
AMY LAURENS

The Quilt-Maker's Scrap
AMY LAURENS